A.R. 7377

BARNES SCHOOL LIBRARY

◁ W9-BEL-500

DATE DUE		
OCT 2 5 2006		
MAR 2 4 2008		
APR 0 6 2009		
MAY 0 4 2009		

DISCARD

E.
BRO   90-100

Brown. Margaret Wise

The Little island

$16.00

BARNES SCHOOL LIBRARY
401 BARNES STREET
KELSO, WA 98626

THE LITTLE ISLAND

by Golden MacDonald

WITH ILLUSTRATIONS BY

Leonard Weisgard

A DOUBLEDAY BOOK FOR YOUNG READERS

BARNES SCHOOL LIBRARY
401 BARNES STREET
KELSO, WA 98626

90-100

Copyright, 1946 by Doubleday & Company, Inc. All Rights Reserved.

There was a little Island in the ocean.

Around it the winds blew

And the birds flew

And the tides rose and fell on the shore.

Clouds passed over it
Fish swam around it
And the fog came in from the sea
and hid the little Island
in a soft wet shadow.

The morning was very quiet
on the Island
with only the spiders sailing their webs
against a gentle wind.

Small flowers, white and blue,
and violets with golden eyes
and little waxy white-pink chuckleberry blossoms
and one tickly smelling pear tree
bloomed on the Island.
And that was the spring.

Then one day
all the lobsters crawled in from the sea
and hid under the rocks and ledges
of the Island to shed their shells
and let their new ones grow hard and strong
in hiding places in the dark.

And the seals came barking down from the north
to lie on the sunny rocks
and raise their baby seals.

And the kingfishers came from the South
to build nests.

And the gulls laid their eggs
on the rocky ledges.

And wild strawberries turned red.
Summer had come to the little Island.

Boats sailed to the little Island
from far away
And herring and mackerel
leaped out of the water
all silver in the moonlight.
The seaweed squeaked at low tide
And little green pears grew on the pear tree.
A black crow flew over.

And a little kitten came to the Island
with some people on a picnic.
The kitten prowled around the Island
And saw that it was all surrounded by water.

"What a little land," said the kitten.
"This little Island is as little
as Big is Big."

BARNES SCHOOL LIBRARY

"So are you," said the Island.
"Maybe I am a little Island too."
said the kitten —
"a little fur Island in the air."
And he left the ground
and jumped in the air.
"That is just what you are,"
said the little Island.

"But I am part of this big world,"
said the little kitten.
"My feet are on it."
"So am I," said the little Island.
"No, you're not," said the kitten.
"Water is all around you
and cuts you off from the land."
"Ask any fish," said the Island.

So the kitten caught a fish.

"Answer me this or I'll eat you up,"

said the kitten.

"How is an Island a part of the land?"

"Come with me," said the fish,

"down into the dark secret places

of the sea and I will show you."

"I can't swim," said the cat.

"Show me another way or I'll eat you up."

"Then you must take it on faith

what I tell you," said the fish

"What's that?" said the cat—"Faith."

"To believe what I tell you

about what you don't know," said the fish.

And the fish told the kitten
how all land is one land
under the sea.
The cat's eyes were shining
with the secret of it.
And because he loved secrets he believed.
And he let the fish go.

And he got on his boat
and sailed away into the setting sun.

The little Island had a little woods on it
with seven big trees in it
and seventeen small bushes
and one big rock.
Birds came to the woods on the Island
And butterflies and moths flew over the ocean
till they got there.

Night came to the little Island
dark and still
And seven little fireflies
flashed in the darkness.
A bat flew
around and around the pear tree
and woke up the owl.
The wind whistled.

Then came the storm.

The wind blew from the South East.

Waves as big as glassy mountains

came before it

And lightning and thunder

And always the howling, moaning, whistling wind.

And then the storm passed

and left the little Island where it found it

in the summer sea.

Autumn came
and the yellow pears dropped
slowly to the ground.

Winter came
and the snow fell softly
like a great quiet secret in the night
cold and still.

Nights and days came and passed

And summer and winter

and the sun and the wind

and the rain.

And it was good to be a little Island.

A part of the world

and a world of its own

all surrounded by the bright blue sea.

A Doubleday Book for Young Readers
Published by Delacorte Press
Bantam Doubleday Dell Publishing Group, Inc.
666 Fifth Avenue, New York, New York 10103

Doubleday
and the portrayal of an anchor with a dolphin
are trademarks of Bantam Doubleday Dell Publishing Group, Inc.

ISBN 0-385-07381-X
Copyright 1946 by
Doubleday & Company, Inc.
All Rights Reserved
Printed in Hong Kong

29 31 33 32 30 28

SCP

BARNES SCHOOL LIBRARY

DISCARD